PLANET IN CRISIS

WATER

SUPPLIES IN CRISIS

This edition published in 2009 by:
The Rosen Publishing Group, Inc.
29 East 21st Street
New York, NY 10010

Copyright © 2009 David West Books

Designed and produced by
David West Books

Editor: James Pickering
Picture Research: Carlotta Cooper

Photo Credits: Abbreviations: t-top, m-middle, b-bottom, r-right,
l-left, c-center.

Front cover, mr & 26bl - Corbis Images. Pages 3 & 27br (Philip Dunn); 4-5, 11bl, 25m (Sipa Press); 9tl (Fotex Medien Agentur GmbH); 12b (MSgt Scott Reed, Airforce photo); 13t (Marius Alexander); 13b (Scott Nelson); 14 (Times Newspapers Ltd); 21t (Miguel Angel Azua Garcia); 21b (Peter Brooker); 24b (Prinsloo); 28br (Ponopresse Internationale); 7b, 12-13t, 15t, 18t - Rex Features Ltd. 4t, 5b, 10-11, 26br, 19b, 22-23, 23t & m, 25b (Mark Edwards); 5t (Gilles Corniere); 6b (Jim Wark); 10 (Dylan Garcia); 25t, 28bl (Gil Moti), 11br (Jorgen Schytte); 12-13b (Herbert Giradet); 14-15 (Glen Christian); 16l (Claes Lofgren); 16r (Ron Giling); 18b (Massimo Lupidi); 19tl (Andre Maslennikov); 19tr (Alex S. Maclean); 20 (Peter Arnold); 20-21 (Hartmut Schwarzbach); 22 (Paul Harrison); 23b (Reinhard Janke); 24t (U.S. Coast Guard, Petty Officer 2nd Class Kyle Niemi); 27t (Paul Howell/ UNEP); 27m (Dan Kamminga); 28-29 (Bojan Brecelj) - Still Pictures. 6t, 7t, 8t, 9tm, 9b, 16-17, 17 all, 26t, 30 - Corbis Images.

Library of Congress Cataloging-in-Publication Data

Parker, Russ, 1970-
  Water supplies in crisis / Russ Parker.
      p. cm. -- (Planet in crisis)
  Includes bibliographical references and index.
  ISBN 978-1-4358-5250-1 (library binding) -- ISBN 978-1-4358-0680-1 (pbk.) -- ISBN 978-1-4358-0686-3 (6-pack)
  1. Water-supply--Juvenile literature. 2. Water use--Juvenile literature. I. Title.
  TD348.P33   2009
  363.6'1--dc22

                                          2008045900

Printed and bound in China

First published in Great Britain by Heinemann Library, a division of Reed Educational and Professional Publishing Limited.

PLANET IN CRISIS
WATER
SUPPLIES IN CRISIS

Russ Parker

rosen publishing's
rosen central

New York

ATLANTA
INTERNATIONAL
SCHOOL.

CONTENTS

The driest places on Earth are deserts, and they are spreading fast. This is partly due to climate change as patterns of rainfall are being altered. It also happens when too many crops are grown and use up the soil's nutrients. The soil turns to sand which cannot absorb water. Instead, it trickles downwards and away.

INTRODUCTION

Water has no shape, color, or smell, and when pure, no taste either. We can see right through it and often hardly notice it. Yet, apart from air, it's the single most important substance for our survival. Indeed all living things, from worms to whales, need regular supplies of it. But there are many problems with it. Some places have far too much and are awash with floods. Other places with too little are barren and lifeless. Much of it is dirty and germ-ridden and spreads disease. We can't live without water, so shouldn't we take better care of it?

Water pollution is a massive problem. Not only does it kill fish and other wildlife, it also contaminates our own supplies.

Many of the rich, industrialized countries have more than enough water. They are able to waste vast amounts without worrying (left). But for poor, developing countries in dry regions (right), water is far from plentiful. It's a vital, scarce, and precious resource that takes much time and effort to obtain.

Water is hardly ever made or destroyed. The same water has been around on Earth for millions of years. And it moves around, too, on a never-ending variety of never-ending journeys called the water cycle.

POWERED BY THE SUN

The movement of water is driven by the heat of the Sun. This warmth, called solar infrared radiation, makes liquid water "disappear." In fact, the liquid water changes into a gas—water vapor. We see this when puddles "dry out" in the Sun.

The water cycle is powered by heat energy from the Sun. It warms or evaporates water into invisible water vapor, which rises into the air. However, air soon becomes cooler with height.

Water frozen as ice in polar ice caps, glaciers, and on mountains is still on the move—but very slowly.

Water flows back to the sea in streams and rivers.

Water returns to the surface by gravity. Droplets in clouds clump together and become heavier until they fall as rain.

Sun's heat evaporates water as vapor from seas and oceans.

Water vapor given off by plants and animals.

So the water vapor condenses, or turns back into liquid, as tiny drops within clouds. The larger drops fall as rain, or fall frozen as sleet, hail, or snow. All these forms of water are called precipitation.

Water vapor condenses into droplets in clouds and eventually falls as rain and snow.

Hot topic

In high mountains, rain and melted snow flow away as gushing rivers, whose moving energy turns turbines for hydroelectric power. But global warming may mean less rain in some areas, so their hydroelectric power stations could become useless.

Melting snow supplies lowland rivers.

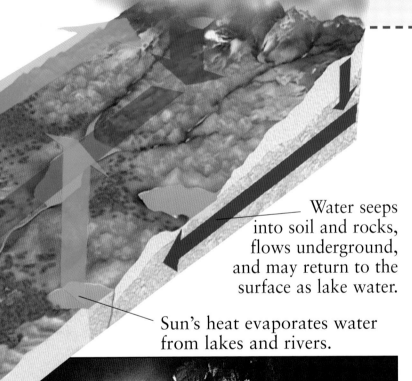

Water seeps into soil and rocks, flows underground, and may return to the surface as lake water.

Sun's heat evaporates water from lakes and rivers.

SALTY TO FRESH

Most water turns into water vapor at the surfaces of seas and oceans. But only the water itself does this. The dissolved form of salts it contains are left behind. So the seas remain salty while the pure water vapor rises into the air. It cools as it gets higher in the winds and turns back into liquid water. This returns to the surface mainly as rain, which flows into streams and rivers, down to the sea— and the cycle continues.

The fresh water we see at the surface is only a tiny amount compared to the water soaked into rocks and flowing in underground rivers and lakes.

WATERY PLANET

Seen from space, planet Earth is mostly covered by water. But nearly all of this is undrinkable salt water in seas and oceans.

SALTY WATER

Salt water is undrinkable, and would kill our farm crops and animals. We need supplies of fresh water, which has very few salts and other minerals dissolved in it.

WHERE WATER IS FOUND

Our planet has plenty of water. Its volume is about 320 million cubic miles; it makes up $1/500$ of the Earth's total weight; and it covers $7/10$ of its surface. However, only 0.01% ($1/10,000$) of all this water is in the form of liquid fresh water at the surface, in lakes and rivers, or in the air. This is called available fresh water, meaning it is available for us to use.

70% Farm crops and animals

Salt water 97.5%

$39/40$ of the Earth's water is salty, in seas, oceans, salty lakes, marshes, and lagoons.

Fresh water 2.5%

Almost $1/3$ of fresh water is underground.

Over $2/3$ of fresh water is frozen as ice.

Available fresh water 0.01%

$2/3$ is in lakes and rivers.

Less than $1/60$ is in plants and animals.

About $1/12$ is in soils.

About $1/8$ is in swamps, marshes, and wetlands.

About $1/10$ is water vapor and clouds in the air.

Less than $1/200$ of all fresh water is available to us, at the surface or in the air.

8% Domestic

22% Industrial

MANY USES FOR WATER

The water which comes out of our taps is only a tiny amount of all the water we use. Most is led along channels, pipes, and ditches to irrigate farm crops in fields and greenhouses. Water is also provided for farm animals to drink and to clean their living places. These agricultural uses account for more than two-thirds of all water used around the world. Another one-fifth of this water is supplied to factories and industrial sites like paper mills and chemical plants.

Water spins turbines at hydroelectric dams like this one in the Oregon town of The Dalles. This use of water energy provides more than one-fifth of all the world's electricity.

Hot topic

In desert regions, water is in short supply. It's especially difficult to grow crops in dry soil. Most years, the majority of people just barely manage. But in drought years, millions may die.

No water = no food

9

Even the driest deserts have some water. But it is usually deep under the ground. To obtain it, people have to dig or drill deep. It's easier to use water at the surface.

SHAPING HISTORY

Easily available surface water has had a huge effect on world history. Most towns and cities grew up on the banks of rivers or lakes, or at estuaries where rivers flow into the sea. Here, fresh water could be used for drinking, cooking, cleaning, watering crops, powering machines like waterwheels, and as transport routes or "highways" for ships and boats.

In dry regions, the main water sources are aquifers—rocks which are slightly porous and hold groundwater like a "stony sponge." These are tapped by drilling shafts called boreholes.

RIVERS AND LAKES

A river is fed by its catchment area. This is where rain, snow, and other precipitation fall and collect into streams, which join the river. Lakes form where the land dips down into a basin, or behind a wall-like dam.

Dry on top, but water below: wind-powered pumps raise groundwater into large storage tanks. These hold enough to last for weeks without wind.

Reservoir behind dam

Lowland lake

Meltwater lake

Crater lake in old volcano

Desert river

Fault

Oasis

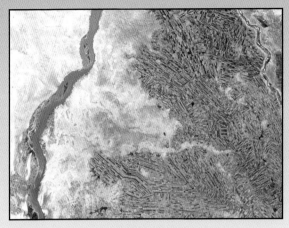

Hot topic
The River Nile in northeast Africa brings life to otherwise parched countries along its banks. But as one nation takes more water for farmland, hydroelectricity, and industry, others have less. "Water War" arguments break out and tensions rise.

The White and Blue Niles (left and upper right) irrigate farms at the edge of the Sahara Desert (left).

UNDERGROUND WATER

The way that water flows and collects is greatly affected by the rocks at or just under the surface. If they are porous (permeable), water can slowly soak in and continue moving underground. Nonporous rocks do not allow this. Water flows over them into streams and smaller rivers (tributaries), which merge into the main river.

Some rain soaks into porous rock and flows underground. The level below, where the rock is saturated or full of water, is called the water table.

Nonporous rock

Porous rock

Water table level

Saturated rock

Oases are pools of water in deserts. They may form where underground water oozes up faults or cracks in the rocks.

Raising or pumping up water from wells and boreholes needs energy. This can come from wind, engines, motors—or muscle power.

11

Water is difficult to transport. It's heavy and bulky; it splashes and sloshes; and it leaks from any tiny crack or hole. But it has one useful feature—it flows.

TRUCKS AND TANKERS

In most places water must be moved from its sources—like rivers, lakes, wells, and reservoirs—to where it's needed. One method is to use water containers, from large trucks and tankers to barrels and buckets. But this takes much time and uses up great energy and effort.

In 2005, after Hurricane Katrina hit New Orleans, Louisiana, drinking water had to be flown in.

Hot topic

Water "mains" are the main pipes to houses and buildings. They are usually underground and their water is under high pressure. Pipes may break for many reasons like freezing, small earth movements, or heavy traffic. Bursts disrupt supplies and even cause local flooding.

An unwanted "fountain"

Cities like London, UK, have water supply pipes below ground, which are emptied for repair (above).

Open channels let water get dirty and evaporate. Pipes keep it clean and reduce loss (below).

MAINS WATER

Most developed countries have mains water supplies with channels, pipes, tubes, and ducts. Water moves along by the force of gravity. In places it must be raised, usually by motorized pumps, so it flows down again and onwards.

In poor areas, collecting water from a shared tap or well is a vital, time-consuming daily job. All family members take a turn.

We turn on the tap, and clean water comes out, safe for drinking and cooking. But for more than two billion people around the world, this "necessity" is a distant dream.

TWO SUPPLIES?

The most important use of water is for drinking, on its own or in juice, coffee, and so on. But this makes up less than one-hundredth of what we use at home. Some people suggest two supplies—one clean and pure, and one less so for utility jobs (below), which would be much cheaper to provide.

When water is scarce and takes time and effort to obtain by hauling it up from a local well, people are much more careful about how they use it.

Many countries charge people for water by the volume they use, measured by a meter. This helps people to be aware of water's worth and always save it.

HOUSEHOLD WATER USE

Washing
34%

Drinking
1%

Utility 65%

Drinking water includes water for cooking. Washing water is for ourselves, our clothes, dishes, and silverware. Utility water is for general cleaning, car-washing, heating systems, houseplants, and gardens.

SAVING WATER

Everyone can save precious water. A bath takes 25 gallons, while a shower only uses 1/3 as much water. A standard flush toilet uses three gallons, a quick-flush half this amount. A dripping tap can waste a gallon in a few hours. "Economy" settings on washing machines and dishwashers save plenty.

HOW MUCH WATER PER PERSON?

Each day at home, a person in a developed country such as the U.S. uses 12 times more water than someone from a developing country. Every drop costs money, time, and energy to purify for use and treat after use, and reduces the amount of available fresh water.

Africa
15
gallons/day

Asia
25
gallons/day

Europe
50 gallons/day

U.S.
80 gallons/day

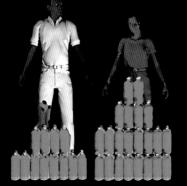

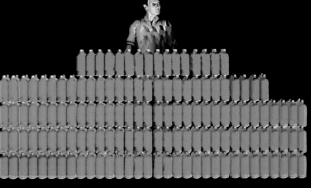

ATLANTA INTERNATIONAL SCHOOL

The water we use at home is only a small amount of the water we consume in other ways. Almost everything we buy, eat, sit on, wear, travel in, and switch on needs water.

MANY TIMES MORE

Every item requires water to manufacture, from obtaining raw materials, to making the machines at the factory, to transporting finished goods to the stores. We do not see these "hidden" uses of water, but they increase our personal use ten times or more.

Electricity for one hour of TV 100 gallons

Power stations need water to cool the high-temperature, high-pressure steam that spins their generators. They are usually built near rivers or the ocean.

One newspape 6 gallons

Making paper and cardboard uses huge amounts of water. One copy of a small newspaper represents six gallons. For a thick weekend newspaper with magazines, this rises to 40 gallons.

A shiny new car does not seem very watery. But all the materials and processes used to manufacture it (below) take up precious water.

One soda can 20 gallons

A soda can made of aluminum holds twelve fluid ounces of liquid—but making it uses 300 times more water.

One car 100,000 gallons

VAST AMOUNTS

It may be difficult to imagine such huge amounts of water. A person in a developed country is responsible, every day, for the use of over 250 gallons of water, which weigh about one ton. Making one small car requires enough water to fill a large swimming pool.

Hot topic

The food industry is one of the biggest consumers of water. It's used to irrigate crops, provide for animals, and wash all produce ready for sale. To make prepared, processed convenience foods, the amounts leap up five or ten times. A pre-washed bag of lettuce requires enough water to fill a garbage can.

Softening tuna fish by steaming

17

Water from our taps is usually safe. But what about water from a dirty brown puddle or a frothy yellow river? It may harbor germs, chemicals, and poisons— but then, so might clear, sparkling water.

Dead fish litter the banks of the River Seine in Paris, France —the result of a chemical spill.

INVISIBLE PROBLEMS

Many substances dissolve and "disappear" into water without trace. We cannot see them, because water is such a good solvent. Yet clear water that looks pure could be swarming with germs and full of toxins. About one-third of the people in the world lack safe drinking water.

A clean river in Italy suddenly became a flowing ribbon of foam. The disaster was due to chemicals from a local factory which, under local laws, were allowed to pour into the water.

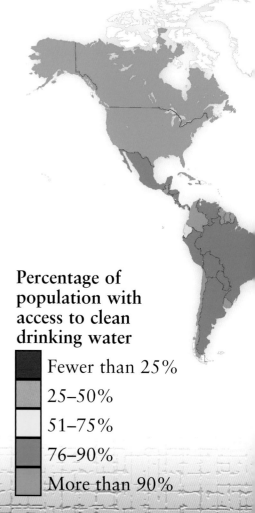

Percentage of
population with
access to clean
drinking water

Fewer than 25%
25–50%
51–75%
76–90%
More than 90%

Water may not be safe even when it falls from the sky. These trees are dying from acid rain.

Hot topic
Nutrients in water feed living things. But too many nutrients from fertilizers or sewage mean that microbes, which are usually rare, breed out of control. This upsets nature's balance and causes toxic "tides" that harm wildlife.

Algal tide, Lake Erie, U.S.

SAFE DRINKING WATER

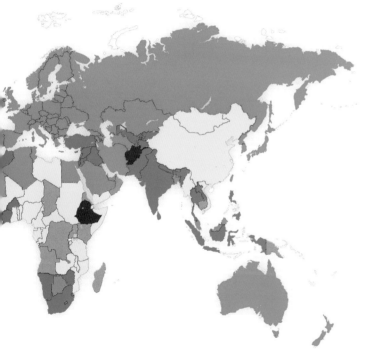

People in rich industrialized countries take clean, pure water for granted. But more than two billion people have little or no access to safe water for drinking and cooking. The most affected countries are in Africa, especially south of the Sahara Desert, where even dirty water is scarce.

GLOBAL PROBLEM

International organizations work to provide clean water for more people. The WaterAid charity aims to help one million people gain access to safe drinking water annually, and a similar number to proper sanitation.

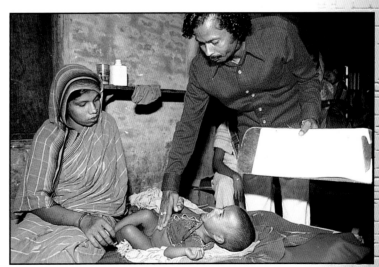

Contaminated water is the source of many deadly diseases such as cholera, dysentery, and typhoid. They kill three million people yearly.

19

Treating water to make it clean, pure, and safe for drinking and cooking is both a complicated technical process and a lucrative business.

NATURAL FILTERS

In general, water from wells, boreholes, and other sources deep in the ground is cleaner than surface water in lakes and rivers. As the water soaks slowly through the rocks, germs and impurities are removed. Water treatment plants use the same process by making water flow slowly through filter beds of gravel and sand.

Water sources, especially rivers, are checked often. In a dry summer, there are more natural impurities.

MAKING PURE WATER

The water supply system cleans water in several stages. Chemicals added in coagulation tanks cause certain impurities to clump together and settle to the bottom. The water trickles into layers of gravel, then sand, which remove more impurities. Added disinfectant chemicals kill any remaining germs before storage.

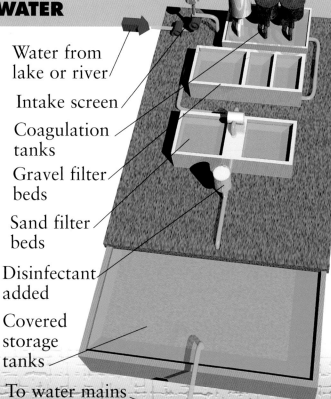

Water from lake or river

Intake screen

Coagulation tanks

Gravel filter beds

Sand filter beds

Disinfectant added

Covered storage tanks

To water mains

Samples of water are taken regularly and tested for levels of harmful chemicals and germs. The amounts of purifying chemicals can be varied, depending on the source, like a well or river.

ADDED TO WATER

Several chemicals might be added to the water in safe amounts. Activated carbon absorbs impurities which may not be harmful, but which would give the water an unpleasant taste or smell. Chlorine may be bubbled through water to help kill germs. In some areas, tiny amounts of added fluoride help teeth to stay strong and healthy and prevent decay.

Tiny amounts of minerals give different sources of water their own tastes. This is especially noticeable in bottled water.

21

Used water that flows away down the drain or toilet does not simply "disappear." It enters a complicated cleaning process at the local water treatment plant.

BACK TO NATURE

At the treatment plant, all kinds of solids and chemicals are removed in a step-by-step process. The aim is to make the water clean enough to flow back into nature, usually into a river or lake.

Reedbeds and marshes are being increasingly used to clean water naturally. The plants' roots filter the water and use its nutrients for growth.

Half the world's people do not have flushing toilets. They use outhouses or even simple holes in the ground, filling them in and changing sites every few days.

SEWAGE

At the treatment plant, used or "foul" water (1) is screened to remove large solids (2). It stands in sedimentation beds (3) where small particles settle out as sludge. "Friendly" bacteria and other microbes breeding in the biological beds (4) are used to kill and remove harmful microbes. This process continues as water trickles from rotating booms in the circular wetbeds (5). The cleaned water flows into a local river (6) while sludge and other leftovers are put into digestion tanks (7). Here they rot and give off the gas methane, which is burned to generate electricity in a power station (8). The final sludge remnants are taken away by road, rail (9), or ship (10) for use as fertilizer.

Being GREEN

Newer methods of water treatment are always being tested. There are several kinds of membrane filtration, where waste water is passed through a special sheet-like membrane to remove impurities. The holes in the membrane can be made to any size, from micro- to nanoscopic.

Membrane filtration

BYPRODUCTS

Along rivers with many towns and cities, it is estimated that the same water is taken out, used, cleaned, and put back in perhaps six or seven times. The byproducts of water treatment include sludges and slurries with many minerals and nutrients. These are allowed to decay or "digest" and produce methane gas, to burn for heat or power.

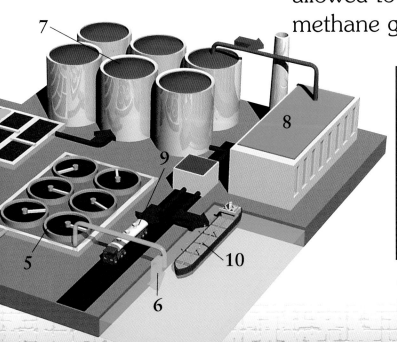

Sludges and slurries from water treatment plants or sewage works are spread on the land as fertilizer, but only after all harmful microbes and chemicals are removed.

23

Each year, water kills several thousand people—not by carrying germs and disease, but by drowning them in floods. The problem of global warming, which is leading to climate change and extreme weather, may increase this terrible toll.

NATURAL OVERFLOW

For thousands of years, most places have coped with their natural amounts of rain and other forms of water. They have rivers and lakes big enough to hold sudden downpours such as tropical monsoon storms.

In 2000, floods covered vast areas of Mozambique, Africa. The waters destroyed buildings, crops, farmland, roads, and electricity supplies.

Hurricane Katrina (see page 12) flooded large areas of the U.S. Gulf Coast, especially New Orleans. More than 1,800 people died in the hurricane itself and in the floods that followed in its aftermath.

Cutting down trees increases flooding. Without tree roots to hold it in place, soil is washed by rain into rivers, where it clogs the channels. Water cannot pass and spills over the land.

Hot topic

Regular small floods can be useful. In parts of India, China, Bangladesh, and Egypt, river flooding spreads silt on the land, in which farm crops thrive. But new dams and irrigation disrupt these age-old occurrences, as in southern China in 2005.

Flood defenses, northern China

CLIMATE CHANGE

Air pollution by "greenhouse gases" is predicted to make world temperatures rise. The gases trap heat in the atmosphere in the same way that glass traps heat in a greenhouse. As a result, some places will not only be warmer, but wetter as well, as patterns of rainfall are altered. This could lead to more storms and devastating floods.

London's Thames River Barrier is a series of "gates" which can be lifted to prevent very high tides from flooding the city. But as sea levels rise with global warming, the barrier may be unable to cope.

Deserts are the driest places on Earth, receiving less than six inches of rain each year. Yet some plants, animals, and even people survive there, suited to conserving water and using it sparingly. Sadly, too many people with modern lifestyles have not adapted in the same way.

North America
The Great Lakes hold one-fifth of the world's surface fresh water. Average levels have fallen by over two feet in 100 years.

WASTING PRECIOUS WATER

Wildlife fits in with its environment. People do the opposite—we change our surroundings to suit ourselves. In places where water is scarce, people are using it thousands of times faster than it can be replenished naturally. Even where water is plentiful, in some big cities more than half is lost through leaks and seepages.

Where water is scarce

■ High population

☐ Low population

Hot topic
On the Colorado River, dams like Glen Canyon in Page, Arizona, and many irrigation pipes reduce the water flow by up to nine-tenths. The habitat for wildlife is so altered that fish like the humpback chub (which lives only here) are at great risk.

Glen Canyon Dam

Central America
Mexico City was once a maze of channels and lakes. So much water has been taken from under the ground that parts of the city have sunk 20 feet in 100 years.

Aral Sea
So much water has been taken from this inland lake, for farms and industry, that its area has been halved in 50 years.

USED TOO FAST

The greatest use for water in dry regions is to irrigate crops. People also want green lawns, wooded parks, swimming pools, fountains, and golf courses. Water for these is raised from boreholes and wells. Such use is not sustainable, as rocks take thousands of years to collect water, and many boreholes run dry in less than ten years.

China
The Three Gorges hydro-electric dam on the Ch'ang Jiang (Yangtze) River, due to begin operating by 2012, is already changing the river in ways no one predicted.

Africa
South of the Sahara, the Sahel area has suffered years of droughts and over-farming. As a result, the once-fertile soil has turned to desert sand.

India
Each monsoon season brings up to 30 feet of rain. But so many farms and people use up the rainwater faster than it can fall.

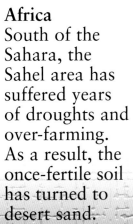

27

The main methods of dealing with water—boreholes, dams, pumps, pipes, purifying it before use, and treating it after—have remained the same for many years. Can any newer technologies help the water crisis?

Desalination is very expensive, both when constructing the pipes, tanks, and machines, and in operating costs.

AIRBORNE WATER

Some places have little surface water, but plenty just above, as fog and mist. In fog collection, large mesh-like sheets are held between tall poles in the drifting fog. Tiny drops gather and merge to make bigger ones that drip into a channel below.

Hot topic

Polar ice is made of highly compressed snow. It melts to give relatively pure water. Suitable-sized icebergs can be located by satellite photographs, hitched by cables, and then towed by boat to warmer regions, where the melting water is collected.

Fog collection was pioneered in Chungungo, a remote village in Chile. Almost 100 collectors gather about 10 gallons of water for each person every day. Before this, the amount available was four gallons.

A captured berg near Greenland

DESALINATION

When the Sun warms the ocean, water vapor evaporates and then condenses as it cools into pure water. This process is copied in desalination, or "de-salting." Ocean water is heated in huge pipes or towers, and the water vapor is captured and condensed into clean, fresh water. Supplies of salty water for this process are almost limitless. But the energy and raw materials needed to build the equipment and heat the water make it costly. Desalination is helpful where desert lands meet the sea, and energy, such as petroleum, is plentiful.

IS RAINMAKING POSSIBLE?

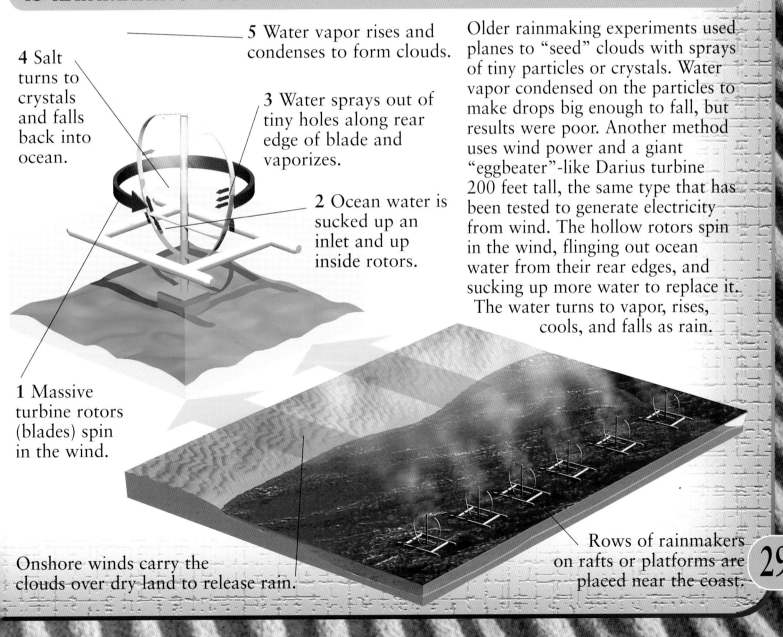

5 Water vapor rises and condenses to form clouds.

4 Salt turns to crystals and falls back into ocean.

3 Water sprays out of tiny holes along rear edge of blade and vaporizes.

2 Ocean water is sucked up an inlet and up inside rotors.

1 Massive turbine rotors (blades) spin in the wind.

Older rainmaking experiments used planes to "seed" clouds with sprays of tiny particles or crystals. Water vapor condensed on the particles to make drops big enough to fall, but results were poor. Another method uses wind power and a giant "eggbeater"-like Darius turbine 200 feet tall, the same type that has been tested to generate electricity from wind. The hollow rotors spin in the wind, flinging out ocean water from their rear edges, and sucking up more water to replace it. The water turns to vapor, rises, cools, and falls as rain.

Onshore winds carry the clouds over dry land to release rain.

Rows of rainmakers on rafts or platforms are placed near the coast.

The world is getting thirstier, as people use more water. In 30 years, half of all people—more than three billion—could face drastic shortages as supplies run out.

EVERYONE CAN HELP

Today, billions must make do with dirty water to wash, cook, and drink. Waterborne diseases kill six people every minute. Wars have been fought over areas that are rich in water. Even you can do something about cutting down on water wastage. Choose showers over baths, turn taps off, and maybe make a poster to encourage others to do the same.

FOR MORE INFORMATION

Organizations

ENVIRONMENTAL PROTECTION AGENCY (EPA) OFFICE OF WATER
Ariel Rios Building
1200 Pennsylvania Avenue, N.W.
Washington, DC 20460
www.epa.gov/ow/
The agency of the federal government of the United States charged with protecting human health and with safeguarding the natural environment.

THE H2O AFRICA FOUNDATION
230 South Elm Street
Zionsville, IN 46077
www.h2oafrica.org
The H2O Africa Foundation is focused specifically on clean water initiatives in Africa.

FRIENDS OF THE EARTH
1717 Massachusetts Avenue,
Suite 600
Washington, DC 20036
(202) 783-7400
www.foe.org/
The largest international network of environmental groups in the world, represented in more than 70 countries, campaigning for a safer, greener future.

SOIL AND WATER CONSERVATION SOCIETY
945 SW Ankeny Road
Ankeny, IA 50023-9723
(515) 289-2331
www.swcs.org/
Soil and Water Conservation Society (SWCS) is a nonprofit scientific and educational organization fostering the science and art of natural resource conservation.

WATERAID AMERICA, INC.
232 Madison Avenue,
Suite 120
New York, NY 10016
(212) 683-0430
www.wateraid.org/usa/
WaterAid is a major charity dedicated to the provision of safe domestic water, sanitation, and hygiene education to the world's poorest people.

For further reading

Bowden, Rob. *Earth's Water Crisis* (What If We Do Nothing?). Strongsville, OH: World Almanac Library, 2007.

Desonie, Dana. *Hydrosphere: Freshwater Systems and Pollution* (Our Fragile Planet). New York, NY: Chelsea House Publications, 2008.

Fine, Jil. *Floods (High Interest Books)*. Danbury, CT: Children's Press, 2007.

Fridell, Ron. *Protecting Earth's Water Supply* (Saving Our Living Earth). Minneapolis, MN: Capstone Press, 2008.

Toupin, Laurie. *Freshwater Habitats: Life in Freshwater Ecosystems*. Danbury, CT: Franklin Watts, 2005.

Woods, Michael and Mary B. *Droughts* (Disasters Up Close). Minneapolis, MN: Lerner Publications, 2006.

Web Sites

Due to the changing nature of Internet links, Rosen Publishing has developed an online list of Web sites related to the subject of this book. This site is updated regularly. Please use this link to access the list:
http://www.rosenlinks.com/pic/wsic

GLOSSARY

catchment area
The area of land which gathers rain and other forms of precipitation for a river.

condense
When the gas called water vapor cools and turns into liquid water.

drought
A long period with little or no rain or other precipitation.

evaporate
When liquid water is heated and turns into a gas called water vapor.

hydroelectricity
Electrical power generated from the energy of running water, usually by a power station at a dam built across a river.

irrigate
To bring water from a river, lake, well, or other source, usually to supply crops and other plants.

oasis
A small place in the desert which has water, usually seeping up from under the ground. Plants grow, and animals and people come to drink.

porous
A substance which has tiny holes, like a bath sponge or certain kinds of rock, allowing water to slowly soak in and flow along.

precipitation
All forms of water that reach the ground from the air, including rain, hail, sleet, snow, dew, fog, mist, and frost.

reservoir
An artificial or human-made lake, usually where water is collected in the river valley behind a dam.

water vapor
Water in the form of a gas, which is invisible and mixes with the other gases in air.

Water supplies in crisis